TAKE A BREATH

Sujean Rim

WISH ME LUCK!

 A CAITLYN DLOUHY BOOK
ATHENEUM BOOKS FOR YOUNG READERS • NEW YORK   LONDON   TORONTO   SYDNEY   NEW DELHI

D1294574

Every morning, all the birds go out to play.
They are excited for their first flight of the day.

All except Bob.

Bob can't quite fly yet.

ALRIGHTY THEN, SEE YOU GUYS LATER.

So he keeps himself busy on the ground . . .

. . . and always practices his flying.

Bob practices a lot.

He understands these things can take time.

Sometimes a lot of time.

NOW THAT'S GONNA LEAVE A MARK.

But it seems the harder he tries . . .

. . . the harder he falls.

OOOOH,
WHAT PRETTY STARS!

Bob starts to get nervous.

WHAT'S WRONG WITH ME?!

He starts to worry
and begins to doubt.

WHY CAN EVERYONE
FLY EXCEPT ME?!

Bob, in fact,

is really freaking out.

WHAT IF I NEVER FLY?!

A passing bird notices.

HEY, YOU OKAY?

SNIFF NOT REALLY.
I CAN'T FLY.

And then Bob just lets it all out.

SO IT'S LIKE MY WINGS DON'T WORK!

I CAN'T **BEGIN** TO TELL
YOU HOW **HARD** I FLAP.

MY TAIL FEATHERS?
YEAH, THEY'RE TUCKED.

UGH. I JUST GOT
MY WINGSPAN CHECKED.
TWICE.

HI, I'M BOB, BY THE WAY.

HI, BOB. I'M CROW. AND I TOTALLY GET IT. I THOUGHT I WOULD **NEVER** PERCH LIKE THE REST OF MY FLOCK. THEY ALL JUST CAWED. IT WAS HUMILIATING.

I CAN'T TELL YOU HOW MANY TIMES I FELL ON MY BEAK AND WANTED TO QUIT. . . . THEN, SOMEHOW, I FIGURED IT OUT.

Crow tells Bob he knows exactly what he needs to do.

OH,
PLEASE—
TELL ME!

Bob thinks Crow must be making fun of him.

Crow insists he isn't.

Crow tells Bob to stand tall but relaxed with his wings by his sides, and continues to give him instructions.

CLOSE YOUR EYES. TRY NOT TO THINK ABOUT FLYING, OR ANYTHING!
BREATHE IN AND OUT THROUGH YOUR BEAK.

BOB! STOP THINKING! GOOD.

NOW, SLOWLY FILL YOUR BELLY WITH AIR.

FILL IT AS MUCH AS YOU CAN . . .
FEELING YOUR FEATHERS FLUFF.

HOLD IT. . . .

NOW LET THE AIR OUT.

H H

Bob is DONE.

But Crow convinces him to try once more.

This time, together. . . .

OKAY, LET'S FIRST RESET AND SHAKE OUT OUR FEATHERS...

SETTLING OUR FEET INTO THE GROUND...LET'S BEGIN TO REACH OUR WINGS
UP TO THE SKY...STRETCHING OUR FEATHER TIPS AWAY FROM OUR TAILS.
KEEP STANDING TALL AND GENTLY FLOAT OUR WINGS BACK DOWN TO OUR SIDES.

NOW, LET'S CLOSE OUR EYES SOFTLY... LETTING GO OF ANY THOUGHTS
OR WORRIES... AND JUST NOTICE OUR BREATH.

LET'S BEGIN TO SLOWLY BREATHE IN AND OUT DEEPLY THROUGH OUR BEAKS.
FILLING OUR BELLIES WITH AIR.... FEELING OUR FEATHERS EXPAND. HOLDING
HERE FOR A MOMENT BEFORE WE SLOOOWLY BREATHE OUT THE AIR ...

LET'S DO THIS A FEW MORE TIMES... INHALE... HOLD... EXHALE....

Bob blinks his eyes open.

He can't believe
how much better he feels.

Bob feels great.

He feels as if he could just
take off and—

Okay, maybe he needs a bit more practice,
but Bob won't doubt himself again.

NICE BREATH, BOB!

Sometimes you just
have to be grounded
before you can fly.

For (human) Bob, Charlie,
Smudge, and Nacho—
the collective heart to my breath

WHAT?! NO NUTS ON THIS FLIGHT?

ATHENEUM BOOKS
FOR YOUNG READERS
An imprint of Simon & Schuster Children's
Publishing Division • 1230 Avenue of the Americas,
New York, New York 10020 • © 2022 by Sujean Rim • Book
design by Lauren Rille © 2022 by Simon & Schuster, Inc. • All
rights reserved, including the right of reproduction in whole or
in part in any form. • ATHENEUM BOOKS FOR YOUNG READERS
is a registered trademark of Simon & Schuster, Inc. Atheneum logo is
a trademark of Simon & Schuster, Inc. • For information about special
discounts for bulk purchases, please contact Simon & Schuster Special Sales
at 1-866-506-1949 or business@simonandschuster.com. • The Simon & Schuster
Speakers Bureau can bring authors to your live event. For more information or
to book an event, contact the Simon & Schuster Speakers Bureau at 1-866-248-3049
or visit our website at www.simonspeakers.com. • The text for this book was set in
Clarendon. • The illustrations for this book were rendered in watercolor, pencil, and digital.
• Manufactured in China • 0122 SCP • First Edition • 2 4 6 8 10 9 7 5 3 1 • Library
of Congress Cataloging-in-Publication Data • Names: Rim, Sujean, author, illustrator. • Title:
Take a Breath / Sujean Rim. • Description: First edition. | New York : Atheneum Books for Young
Readers, [2021] | "A Caitlyn Dlouhy Book." | Audience: Ages 4–8. | Audience: Grades K–1. | Summary:
Bob the bird keeps trying to fly, but is beginning to worry that he will never succeed when Crow comes
by with a suggestion to "take a breath." • Identifiers: LCCN 2020056070 (print) | LCCN 2020056071 (ebook)
| ISBN 9781534492530 (hardcover) | ISBN 9781534492547 (ebook) • Subjects: CYAC: Birds—Fiction. | Flight—
Fiction. | Breathing exercises—Fiction. | Relaxation—Fiction. | Self-confidence—Fiction. • Classification:
LCC PZ7.R4575 Bre 2021 (print) | LCC PZ7.R4575 (ebook) | DDC [E]—dc23 • LC record available at
https://lccn.loc.gov/2020056070 • LC ebook record available at https://lccn.loc.gov/2020056071